Hunter's Moon

Paul Blum

RISING★STARS

NASEN House, 4/5 Amber Business Village, Amber Close,
Amington, Tamworth, Staffordshire, B77 4RP

Rising Stars UK Ltd.
7 Hatchers Mews, Bermondsey Street, London SE1 3GS
www.risingstars-uk.com

Published 2012
Reprinted 2015

Cover design: Burville-Riley Partnership
Brighton photographs: iStock
Illustrations: Chris King for Illustration Ltd (characters and cover artwork)/
Abigail Daker (map) http://illustratedmaps.info
Text design and typesetting: Geoff Rayner
Publisher: Rebecca Law
Editorial manager: Sasha Morton Creative Project Management

British Library Cataloguing in Publication Data.
A CIP record for this book is available from the British Library.

ISBN: 978-0-85769-599-4

Printed and bound by Ashford Colour Press Ltd.

Contents

Name:
John Logan

Age:
24

Hometown:
Manchester

Occupation:
Author of
supernatural
thrillers

Special skills:
Not yet known

profiles

Name:
Rose Petal

Age:
22

Hometown:
Brighton

Occupation:
Yoga teacher, nightclub and shop owner, vampire hunter

Special skills:
Private investigator specialising in supernatural crime

Location map

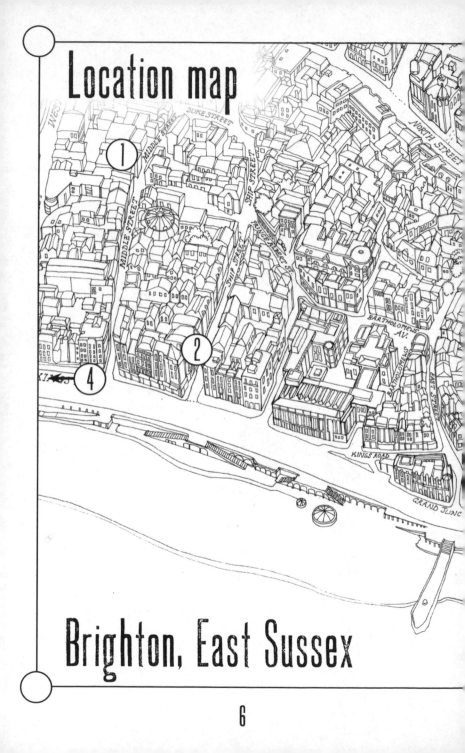

Brighton, East Sussex

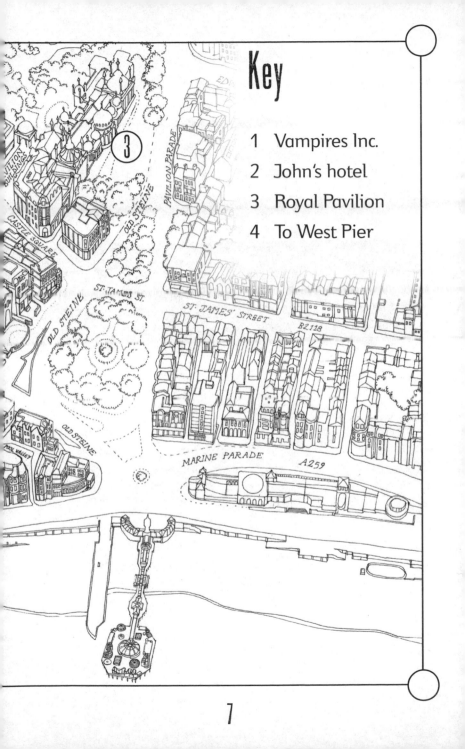

Key

1 Vampires Inc.
2 John's hotel
3 Royal Pavilion
4 To West Pier

Chapter 1

Jack Grey heard the door to the nearby toilet open. He looked around at the person behind him. Dark eyes looked into his. Pale hands went to his shoulders. Sharp teeth sank into his neck. It was over quickly.

The man with the dark eyes left the toilets and walked onto the beach. Pebbles crunched under his feet. One foot dragged as the killer limped away from his victim.

The late summer moon was out before the sun had set. They called this a Hunter's Moon, and this hunter had already found its prey.

****

Earlier that day, John Logan had jumped into a taxi at Brighton train station. He checked his reflection in the window. A smart, good-looking man in his twenties looked back at him. It was a lovely summer afternoon in Brighton. Most people were dressed in cool clothes. Some had colourful hair, piercings and tattoos.

John Logan was a writer. His first book was about vampires and it had been a big hit. Now he planned to write another. Brighton had always been an important place for those who believed in the supernatural. People who believed they were wizards or witches lived and worked here. It was the perfect place for John's research.

He even had a new contact in Brighton to help him with it.

The taxi dropped John at his hotel. He checked into his room, locked up his laptop and walked back into town to meet his new research assistant.

In an alley just off Middle Street, John heard the sound of bells. Wind chimes were swinging from every door and window. He stopped at a red door. The sign read 'Vampires Inc.'.

John stepped inside the small shop. There were candles everywhere but it was still very dark. A strong smell of perfumed oil filled the air.

A young woman sat on a rug. She was chanting softly and her eyes were closed. 'Omm, omm,' she said.

'Hi, I'm John Logan,' he said. 'Are you Rose?'

'I'm busy,' she whispered. 'Wait for me upstairs.'

John didn't know what to say. He walked up a narrow set of stairs into a dark room with more candles. Without warning, something flew out of the shadows. It missed his head by inches. Before he could stop himself, John let out a yell.

'Don't worry about Danny,' called the woman. 'He's just being friendly. Stay still and he'll leave you alone.'

John turned to see a big white owl looking at him with bright green eyes. This place is really odd, he thought.

Shortly, the woman ran up the stairs.

'I'm Rose Petal,' she said. 'It's nice to meet you. I run yoga classes up here during the day. Downstairs is my little shop and in the basement is my bar and nightclub.'

Rose Petal wore black from head to toe. She had bright red hair, at least ten earrings in each ear and a tiger tattoo on one shoulder. She flicked a switch to turn on some lights. 'Beads, necklaces, black clothes ... I sell everything for fashionable vampires and their friends,' she said.

John Logan looked around him and grinned. 'You're talking about vampires as if they're real,' he said.

Rose gave John a long, hard stare.

'You wouldn't want to work with me

if vampires weren't real.'

Then Rose clicked her fingers and the white owl landed on her arm. 'So have you come to talk about your book, or what? My next yoga class starts in ten minutes.'

John felt himself getting cross. 'I need more than ten minutes,' he snapped. 'You emailed me. You wanted to be my research assistant. I'm here to start writing.'

Rose shrugged her shoulders and gave him a business card. 'Something came up,' she said.

He read the card with a grin on his face. 'This says you're a private investigator. You do that as well as all these other jobs?'

ROSE PETAL VAMPIRES INC.

Private investigator

Specialising in the unexplained

0888 000666   rp1@666.br.uk

'Yeah,' she replied. 'I help a police inspector who wants to know about Brighton's vampires. A murder case came up last night. It's a vampire killing. You can either help me with it or you can carry on making up stories. That's the type of research assistant I am. I'll show you the truth. What do you think?'

John thought she was crazy. But she just might give him an idea for his new book. 'I'm in,' he said. 'Tell me what's going on.'

'Read these,' said Rose, handing him a pile of folders. The top one said 'Police Report'. 'I'll call you later when you've done your research.'

Chapter 2

That evening, John sat up late reading the files Rose had given to him. They described a world he would never have believed was real. It was dark when he put the files down.

John looked out of his hotel window at the waves crashing onto the beach. He could see the bright lights of Brighton Pier and hear people chatting and laughing outside. Surely this was just another seaside town?

'So Brighton has become a centre for the supernatural,' he read out.

POLICE RESEARCH DOCUMENT, CONTINUED

Vampire interview #75

"Vampires like Brighton because of its bars and night-life. It's a city full of young people having fun. But most importantly, it is a tolerant city. You can be who you really are in Brighton, no questions asked!"

John flung down the papers on the bed. 'This is mad,' he thought. 'No-one actually believes vampires, ghosts and werewolves are real. This is a waste of time.'

Just then John's phone rang, making him jump. It was Rose Petal. She spoke quickly and quietly.

'John, it's me. Meet me at the sea-front toilets near the West Pier. They've found another body.'

It was midnight when John arrived at the pier. The police had closed off the area, but they let Rose through when they saw her. John was surprised, but followed her. Inside the toilets, a man's body lay in front of the sinks.

'Who is he?' John asked.

'Jack Grey,' she said. 'He was a history student. A witness saw a man coming out of these toilets at about eight o'clock. He was limping badly,' said Rose. 'Look at those marks on his neck.'

'A knife wound? Needle marks?' asked John.

Rose shook her head. 'Those are bite marks,' she said.

John was silent. He didn't want to admit it, but Rose was right.

Chapter 3

John and Rose met up the next day at the hospital café. John was surprised to see Rose wearing a doctor's white coat.

'Were you at the post-mortem?' he asked.

'I'm always there when there are bite marks of any kind,' she explained. 'A few years ago, I solved some murder cases that the police wanted to keep quiet. This town relies on tourists — no one will visit a place where you might get killed. In Brighton we have a few rules that the vampires and werewolves follow, but sometimes things go wrong. The police trust me to put things right.'

'You did just say "werewolves", didn't you?' asked John. He couldn't believe what he was hearing.

'Yes, John. Vampires, werewolves and all kinds of other creatures live here. The more you know about all of this, the safer you'll be.'

'I see,' John said, trying to keep his voice calm. He didn't want her to see how scared he was. This was actually happening. It wasn't just some weird dream. Vampires did exist!

Rose carried on speaking. 'The bite marks on Jack Grey's neck are the same as bite marks we found on two other girls. Their bodies were found in the grounds of the Royal Pavilion.'

'But this body was found by the

beach,' said John. 'Is there a link?'

Rose shrugged. 'I don't know yet. But I know someone who might. Come to the club tonight.'

Chapter 4

John arrived at Vampires Inc. at 10pm. The bar and dance floor were packed. It was full of people wearing dark make-up and black clothes.

'Hi John,' called Rose from behind the bar. 'Are you ready for your first night out with the undead?'

He looked round the room. He had never felt more uncomfortable in his life. 'How can you tell the vampires and the humans apart?' John shouted over the music.

'Years of practice,' she said. 'Don't worry, they've all had dinner. You're safe!'

As Rose led him across the dance floor, a vampire girl grabbed his arm. John's heart jumped in fright as she shouted, 'Are you the new man in Rose's life?'

John felt himself blushing. Rose pulled him away. 'Sorry about that,' she said.

'It's Brighton,' he said, nervously. 'Anything goes, right?'

Rose Petal took him into a room behind the dance floor. 'I want you to meet Rodney, my contact,' she said.

John's mouth fell open. Rodney was the hairiest man he had ever seen. Rose saw the look of surprise on John's face and grinned. 'Rodney is half werewolf, but he's also a great fortune-teller. He can see into the past as well as into the future.'

'You can trust in me and my crystal ball,' said Rodney. He put his hands on the glass ball. It started to glow and the room lit up. Rodney began to shake and his eyes rolled back in his head. Suddenly, he sat bolt upright.

'I see two hundred years ago as if it were today. The mirror, the tunnel. Water is the healer. But the doctor hides his true face. He drinks blood, not water,' growled Rodney.

He stopped, then closed his eyes. Rodney seemed to go into a deep sleep. Slowly, Rodney's yellow eyes opened. 'Did I do well?' he asked.

'You did very well,' Rose said,

squeezing his hand. 'Thank you. Come on, John. We need to go.'

John was silent as they left the club, but his mind was racing. He and Rose went out into the street.

'What's going on?' asked John.

'Rodney speaks in riddles but I know what he meant,' she said. 'We need to visit a man called Ben Kent. He lives near the Royal Pavilion. He was teaching Jack Grey on the day he died. I've been keeping an eye on him for a while. I think he knows more than he told the police.'

Chapter 5

Ben Kent was a very tall, handsome
man with white hair. He had an office
in the grounds of Brighton's Royal
Pavilion. It was past midnight, but he
let Rose and John inside straight away.

'You're working late, Dr Kent,' said
Rose Petal, looking around the room.
Dr Kent's desk was piled high with
paper.

'Yes, I do my best work at night,' he
said. 'I lost some time today talking to
the police about Jack's death.'

'Were you with Jack Grey on the day
he died?' asked John. 'Did he seem

worried about anything?'

'No, he was a very good student,' replied Ben Kent. 'Who are you, exactly?'

'This is my friend, John. He's just here for a holiday,' said Rose quickly. 'By the way, Dr Kent, how's your limp?'

'Not great,' he said, before he could stop himself.

Rose looked at him and smiled. Ben Kent went very pale.

'I'm so sorry to hear that. Thank you for your help, Dr Kent. We won't keep you any longer. We'll show ourselves out. Goodbye.'

They were almost at the front door when Rose pushed John into a small office.

'What are you doing? Let's go!' cried John.

Rose ignored him. She was sliding her hand along the frame of a huge mirror. Suddenly, there was a click and the mirror swung open to reveal a secret passage. John gasped.

'How did you know that was there?'

'I did my research,' replied Rose. She led the way down the passage, using her phone as a torch. After five minutes, they arrived in front of a row of wooden boxes, covered in dust.

'Coffins,' she said. 'Do something useful, John. Open one of them, while I read this wall chart.'

'What with?' he asked. 'My bank card?'

'Try this.' Rose threw him a crowbar from her rucksack. 'It's good to be ready for anything here.'

John pulled out the rusty nails and lifted the lid of the coffin. A skeleton lay inside. John gagged and pushed the lid back down.

Rose shone the light onto a list on the wall. 'Everyone that Dr Kent has killed is on this list. It goes back nearly two hundred years, to 1822. It would seem that Ben Kent is a vampire who used to pretend to be a famous healer,' she explained.

'Rodney said that in his riddle,' John gasped. '"Water is the healer. But the doctor hides his true face."'

'Dr Benjamin Kent was King George the Fourth's doctor, over two hundred years ago. Kent was famous for getting people to drink seawater and swim here to make them well. There are lots of secret passages under the Royal Pavilion. I think Dr Kent uses them to move about in the daylight and look for his victims. One of them probably leads to the part of the beach where Jack was killed. He must have found out about his teacher's secret.'

A door slammed and then there was silence.

'It sounds like Dr Kent's left the house. What happens next? Do we call the police?' asked John, hoping that Rose wouldn't follow the vampire.

'Vampires love to kill under a Hunter's Moon, like the one tonight. It makes them even stronger. I think Dr Kent is going back to the beach to hunt. I've seen the old Royal Pavilion plans. This tunnel should lead us to the beach. Let's go!' Rose cried.

Chapter 6

Rose and John ran down the tunnel.
It twisted and turned, but they soon
found themselves on the beach. Rose
ran ahead. The stones crunched loudly
under her feet.

John called out for her to stop and
she turned. A shadow moved behind
her. Rose shivered. Something didn't
feel right ...

It was Dr Kent. He grabbed Rose
Petal and held her tightly. 'I wondered
when you would get here,' he laughed.

'Leave her alone!' John shouted. 'You
won't get away with this!'

Rose shook her head at John, and looked up at the sky. Dark clouds were clearing and the moon was bright. Dr Kent grinned as he looked up at the moon. His pointed teeth shone in the light.

Rose twisted around and whispered in his ear. His eyes grew wide. He let her go and started to back away. John could see fear on his face. Then, Dr Kent started running across the beach towards the sea.

His limp and the stones slowed him down. Rose took a wooden stake from her bag. She caught up with the vampire easily. Swiftly, she used the stake to stab the doctor in the back. There was a scream, and then Ben Kent was nothing but dust.

'What did you do? Where did he go?' shouted John.

'I called him by his first name three times,' she said, rubbing grey dust from her black clothes. 'That's how you get a vampire to follow your command. Then I told him to run into the sea. He was never going to get away from me. Job done: one less vampire to worry about.'

For the second time that day, John couldn't believe what he was hearing. 'But he should be put in prison. You can't just kill people!'

Rose laughed. 'Have you ever tried to put a two-hundred-year-old vampire behind bars? It just doesn't seem to scare them,' she said. 'He broke the rules that all the other vampires here live by. I stopped him. That's my job.'

With that, Rose started walking back up the beach. John stood for a while, taking deep breaths. Then he slowly followed Rose back to the bar.

****

John had so many questions. He opened up his laptop to write, but Rose shook her head. 'It's too late, we'll start work tomorrow.'

Danny, the white owl, flew over to the table to watch John sip a glass of water. John was too tired to be scared of the bird any more.

'Danny seems to like you,' smiled Rose. 'I guess you'll have to stay here after all. Let's see how quickly we can get that new book written. Then you can go back to your normal life.'

John smiled and put out his hand. The owl's head was warm and furry. Perhaps it wasn't such a bad creature. Maybe in the morning, all of this would make sense. He had seen a whole new world. And although he couldn't believe everything about it yet, he wanted to be part of it.

Glossary

nightclub – a place where people go at night to dance and meet friends

post-mortem – an examination of a body to find out the cause of death

research assistant – person who will find out information on a particular topic

Royal Pavilion – an Oriental-style palace in Brighton built by King George the fourth in the early 19th century

supernatural – events or beings that can't be explained scientifically, such as ghosts, vampires or werewolves

Quiz

1 Who was killed on Brighton beach?

2 Name the writer who has travelled to Brighton.

3 What was the subject of the writer's first book?

4 Who owns the shop and club called Vampires Inc.?

5 What colour does the owner of Vampires Inc. wear all the time?

6 Which type of animal lives at Vampires Inc.?

7 Why do supernatural creatures like living in Brighton?

8 What was found on Jack Grey's neck?

9 Who uses a crystal ball?

10 What was the name of Jack Grey's killer?

Quiz answers

1 Jack Grey

2 John Logan

3 Vampires

4 Rose Petal

5 Black

6 A white owl

7 It is a tolerant city with a good nightlife

8 Bite marks

9 Rodney

10 Dr Ben Kent